Lily

Saddle Up Series
Book 38

Dave and Pat Sargent are longtime residents of Prairie Grove, Arkansas. Dave, a fourth-generation dairy farmer, began writing in early December 1990. Pat, a former teacher, began writing shortly after. They enjoy the outdoors and have a real love for animals.

Lily

Saddle Up Series
Book 38

By Dave and Pat Sargent

Beyond "The End"
By Sue Rogers

Illustrated by Jane Lenoir

Ozark Publishing, Inc.
P.O. Box 228
Prairie Grove, AR 72753

Cataloging-in-Publication Data

Sargent, Dave, 1941–
    Lily / by Dave and Pat Sargent ;
illustrated by Jane Lenoir.—Prairie Grove, AR :
Ozark Publishing, c2004.
    p. cm. (Saddle up series ; 38)

    "A second chance"—Cover.
    SUMMARY: When Lily the lilac dun
and two or three of her closest horse friends
are horsenapped from the Rocking S horse
ranch, she gets a new lady boss who goes
by the name of Belle Starr. Includes factual
information about lilac dun horses.
    ISBN 1-56763-697-7 (hc)
            1-56763-698-5 (pbk)

    1. Horses—Juvenile fiction. [1. Horses—
Fiction. 2. Ranch life—Fiction. 3. Starr,
Belle, 1848–1889—Fiction.] I. Sargent,
Pat, 1936– II. Lenoir, Jane, 1950– ill.
III. Title. IV. Series.

    PZ7.S2465Lh 2004
    [Fic]—dc21   2001005618

Inspired by

lilac duns we see as we travel to schools all across the United States.

Dedicated to

Miss Faith London Finklea, our new granddaughter, born June 23, 2002. We know that Faith loves horses. Her nursery is full of rocking horses!

Foreword

When Lily the lilac dun and two or three of her closest horse friends are horsenapped from the Rocking S Horse Ranch, she gets a new lady boss. Lily likes her boss, who goes by the name of Belle Starr.

Contents

If you would like to have the authors of the Saddle Up Series visit your school, free of charge, call 1-800-321-5671 or 1-800-960-3876.

One

The Outlaws' Hideout

The sound of horses' hooves thundered against the silence of the night. Light from the full moon cast shadows beneath the trees and the small foliage as the terrified horses tried to outrun the outlaws who were chasing them. Lily the lilac dun stumbled over a rock and fell. The blue roan, running directly behind her, had to leap over her.

Lily jumped up and caught up with the others. "I'm frightened. I wonder what are these men going to

1

do with us?" she asked breathlessly.

"I don't know," the blue roan groaned. "Probably they're going to take us to their hideout until the men from the Rocking S Horse Ranch stop looking for us."

One hour later, the small band of stolen horses was herded through an open gate and into a pole corral.

"Oh mercy," Lily Lilac Dun groaned as the gate closed behind them. "Our ranch boss will never find us here. I'm not sure that I could even find my way home after traveling over all of those hills and through the trees."

"Don't worry your pretty head, Lily," the appaloosa said quietly. "We'll take care of you."

"Right," the blue roan agreed. "The outlaws have gone into the cabin for the night. Try to get some sleep. Maybe we can figure out what to do in the morning."

A tear trickled down Lily's face, and she quickly wiped it off on her knee.

"You're right," she said quietly. "There's nothing we can do about our problem tonight." She looked at the blue roan and the appaloosa before adding, "But tomorrow we'll figure out some way to get back to the Rocking S."

Murmurs of agreement echoed amid the little band of stolen horses.

"Thanks, fellows," she said. "Now let's try to get some sleep."

The sun was peeking over the eastern horizon as Lily the lilac dun opened her pretty eyes and yawned. "Hmmm," she thought. "Nothing looks familiar. Where am I?"

"Oh dear. Now I remember!" she groaned. "Outlaws stole us from the Rocking S Horse Ranch last night."

"Easy, Lily," a deep voice said.

She glanced over her shoulder.
Blue Roan was walking slowly
toward her.

"We'll just stay calm," he said. "We'll soon find out what the horse thieves have in mind for us."

Suddenly a man and a woman came out of the cabin and hurried toward the corral. Lily watched them laughing and talking as they opened the gate.

"They sure don't sound mean," she murmured. "Maybe everything will be okay."

The man pointed to Lily and smiled. "Belle," he said quietly, "this is the horse for you. She's a pretty little mare with a lot of sense."

The woman calmly approached the lilac dun. Lily whinnied as Belle stroked her gently on the neck.

"Oh, she's beautiful, Sam," Belle said. "I think we'll get along real good. Don't you?"

"That depends," the lilac dun thought. "I don't know a thing about being an outlaw horse."

Sam put his arm around Belle's shoulder and then quietly said, "She's your wedding gift from me, Belle." He paused before adding, "That is, if you agree to marry me."

"Huh?" Lily murmured. "Did I hear him right? I never heard of an outlaw getting married. Interesting! Maybe this new boss lady will settle down and raise a good family."

"Why, Sam Starr," Belle said. "I never thought I would consider marrying an Irish Cherokee." She smiled and added, "But I will."

"Well, doggone," the blue roan muttered. "I thought anything may happen in an outlaw hideout, but I sure wasn't expecting a marriage."

"Me either," Lily said with a giggle. "But really, it's pretty neat, isn't it?"

The stolen horses nodded their heads in agreement as Belle and Sam left the corral.

Two

Boss Belle Starr

The first day at the outlaws' hideout was very calm and quiet. The Rocking S horses spent most of the day watching for trouble and wondering about their future. Late in the afternoon, Sam and three other men entered the corral.

"Oh dear," the lilac dun said with a sigh. "I hope they let us stay together."

"Maybe they will, Lily," the blue roan whispered. "Let's be calm and listen to their plans."

Sam pointed to the lilac dun and said, "That is Belle's horse, men. And I like the looks of that blue roan for myself."

"Psst, Blue Roan. Did you hear that?" Lily nickered softly, "It sounds like we get to stay together."

The blue roan grinned. "It sure does, Lily," he replied. "I'm happy about that."

A tall slim man walked over to the appaloosa and patted him on the neck.

"One thing's for sure, Sam," he said with a chuckle. "Every horse from the Rocking S is better than the ones we've been riding."

Later that night Lily heard the corral gate open and quietly close. A moment later, Belle walked up to her and whispered, "I can't go to sleep. I thought it might help if I spent some time with you."

"I'm glad you're here," Lily nickered softly.

"My life," Belle said as she stroked the lilac dun on the nose, "has been pretty wild. I was married to Jim Reed for a while. But he rode with Quantrill's gang and was shot by a lawman. It seems like I always end up with men on the wrong side of the law."

"Sam Starr seems nice," Lily murmured.

"Maybe Sam and I," Belle said, "will be able to stay honest. Maybe stealing you and your friends will be our last dishonest deed."

Lily heard a big chuckle and glanced around. The sorrel was pawing at the dirt with his hoof.

"Just why are you laughing?" Lily asked gruffly.

14

"They may not know many honest folks," he said with a laugh. "It's a pretty big challenge to change old habits."

"I think Belle and Sam are nice," Lily said harshly.

Belle smiled and offered a sugar cube to the lilac dun. The mare gently picked it up with her upper lip and smiled.

"Really nice," she murmured. "Thanks, Boss."

Several weeks passed with Lily and Belle exploring the hills near the hideout. The lilac dun soon learned that her boss was an expert rider and a crack shot with a gun. The two of them spent many happy calm and wonderful hours together.

Late one evening Belle was unsaddling Lily when Sam arrived at her side.

"Tomorrow is the day, Belle," he said with a smile. "Are you ready for our wedding?"

"Yes," Belle said. "I'm ready, but I wish we had more friends to help us celebrate our union."

Sam looked stern and shook his head. "You know we have to be careful, little gal. We'll have a few good friends whom we can trust."

"Yes," she answered quietly.

"I understand. The penalty for horse stealing is severe."

The following morning, Lily felt proud as her boss stepped from the cabin to join the little group of outlaws gathered nearby. "Hmmm," the lilac dun thought. "Those folks don't look mean!"

"Boss," she whinnied softly. "You look beautiful!"

Belle smiled at Lily and then stopped at Sam's side.

The ceremony was short, and the little band of outlaws cheered as the bride and groom turned around to face them as man and wife for the first time.

"Okay, Boss," she whispered. "Now you can start a new honest life as Boss Belle Starr." Lily wiped a tear from her face on one knee.

Belle glanced at Lily with a wink and a nod of her head.

Three

The Fertile Valley

Four days later, sudden gunfire thundered over the hideout cabin, shattering the morning peace.

"What's happening?" Lily the lilac dun nickered.

"The ranch hands from the Rocking S found us," the blue roan neighed. "Stay back from the fence, Lily. You could get hurt."

"Oh dear," Lily murmured. "I like the fellows from the Rocking S, but I don't want them to hurt my new lady boss."

"I feel the same way, Lily," Blue Roan groaned. "Boss Sam has become a good friend of mine."

Suddenly Lily lunged forward and soared over the pole fence.

"I have to save my boss," she nickered as she loped toward the cabin amid the shower of bullets.

"Come back!" the blue roan neighed. "You'll get hurt!"

But the lilac dun did not slow down. The blue roan shook his head, then he leaped over the fence.

"You're right!" he snorted. "Let's save our bosses!"

Lily neighed loudly as she came to a skidding halt beside the cabin. A second later, Belle ran out of the door and leaped onto her back.

"Hang on, Boss," Lily said through clenched teeth. "I'm going to make tracks away from here."

"No, wait!" Belle exclaimed. "I don't want to leave Sam here."

Lily glanced back as she raced through the dense forest.

"Don't you worry about Sam," she nickered. "Blue Roan and his boss are right behind us."

Throughout the long day, Lily and the blue roan traveled hard and fast. They walked on the rocks to hide their tracks, and as the sun slowly crept toward the western horizon, they swam across a river.

"I think we've lost the ranch hands from the Rocking S, Boss," Lily nickered. She was exhausted, and so were the others. She stumbled up the bank of the river.

"Sam," Belle said. "We must stop for the night. Our horses are exhausted, and so am I."

In the night, as Belle and Sam slept, Lily and Blue Roan rested and talked about the events of the day.

"I think we did the right thing, don't you?" Lily asked.

"Yes," the blue roan agreed. "We helped our bosses escape. I feel we did the right thing."

Lily sighed and whispered, "At least the other horses will return to the Rocking S Horse Ranch."

"You're right, Lily," Blue Roan agreed. He chuckled as he added, "And you and I will experience a lot of exciting times."

"I sure hope not!" Lily said. "I'm ready for some peace and quiet. Maybe Boss will settle down now."

Fourteen days later, Lily was traveling alongside Blue Roan when Belle suddenly reined her to a halt.

Belle sat and stared at Sam for a moment before saying, "I'm tired of running, Sam. We need a home."

The Irish Cherokee nodded his head. After removing his hat, he wiped his brow with one hand.

"You're right, Belle. We need to settle down in one spot."

"Yes!" Lily neighed. "Now you're talking horse sense."

The blue roan smiled and then snorted, "What's the matter, Lily? Don't you like being an outlaw horse?"

"No, I don't," the lilac dun said. "It's a scary, tiring, and hungry way of life."

Belle Starr and Sam nudged the horses forward with the heels of their boots.

"Where are we?" Belle asked as they rode to the top of a hill.

"Indian Territory," Sam said. He pointed down toward a green and lush valley and asked, "What do you think, Belle? Shall we build our ranch right there?"

"Yes," she said quietly.

"Yes," the blue roan nickered.

"Yes!" Lily neighed loudly.
"Let's build a ranch right there."

"Hmmm," the lilac dun thought as she walked toward the fertile valley. "I sure hope Boss is on the side of the law from now on. Belle Starr has a chance to start an honest life in ranching. She'll be remembered by folks as a colorful character."

"But," Lily added aloud, "I just wonder if anybody will remember her little lilac dun named Lily." Then she whinnied thoughtfully, "Hmmm. It doesn't really matter. Life is one big exciting adventure!"

Four

Lilac Dun Facts

The term *dun* is used in a general sense to describe lighter horse colors, some of which do not have black points.

Years ago, duns without black points were split into red duns and yellow duns which included claybank duns and palominos.

The lilac dun is a very rare horse color that does not fit well into the red dun/yellow dun groups. Lilac dun horses have chocolate brown points and a lilac-colored body. The skin of the lilac dun is light brown or pink, and the eyes are usually amber.

Lilac Dun

BEYOND "THE END"

Horses give us the wings we lack.

Anonymous

WORD LIST
lilac dun
colic
Palomino
muzzle
laminitis
blue roan
body brush
pneumonia
sorrel
ear tips
Pinto
tail
tetanus
sweat scraper
lower legs
equine flu

hoof oil and brush
Appaloosa
mane comb
grey sabino
thrush
mane

From the word list above, write:

1. Three color names for horses and ponies that are recognized as breeds in the United States.
2. Four words that name colors of horses.
3. Four words that name grooming equipment.
4. Five extremities, or points, of a horse that are sometimes a darker color than the rest of its body. What color are Lily's points?
5. Six words that name common illnesses.

Describe these illnesses. Tell the symptoms a horse might show that indicate each illness.

CURRICULUM CONNECTIONS

Did you know horses use their tails to send signals to each other about how they are feeling? How else is a horse's tail useful to him or her in the summer? How is it useful in the winter?

Learn more about Belle Starr at <www.outlawsandlawmen.homestead.com/BelleStarr.html>.

What name did Belle Starr's parents give her at birth? How did Belle Starr die? Belle was drawn to men who robbed trains and banks, rustled cattle, and stole horses—outlaws of the old west! She led such an adventurous life that a newspaper man was inspired to write a book about her after her death. He stretched the facts of her life so much that it has become hard to separate truth from legend. The book sold for twenty-five cents.

A horse walks at the rate of four miles an hour, trots at nine miles, and gallops at twelve. When Lily and her new boss stopped running from the men from the Rocking S Horse Ranch, they trotted for two hours and walked for one hour before they stopped. How many miles did they travel after they stopped running?

PROJECT

Combine your math and artistic skills! Draw to scale and accurately color a picture (body, tail, and mane) of the horse that is featured in each book read in the Saddle Up Series. You could soon have sixty horses prancing around the walls of your classroom!

Learning + horses = FUN.

Look in your school library media center for books about how to draw a horse and the colors of horses. Don't forget the useful information in the last chapter of this book (Lilac Dun Facts) and the picture on the book cover for a shape and color guide.

HELPFUL HINTS AND WEBSITES

A horse is measured in hands. One hand equals four inches. Use a scale of 1" equals 1 hand.

terms, tack & equipment, breeds, art & graphics, and much more information Visit website <www.equisearch.com> to find a glossary of equine terms, information about tack and equipment, breeds, art and graphics, and more about horses. Learn more at <www.horse-country. com> and at <www.ansi.okstate.edu/ breeds/horses/>. KidsClick! is a web search for kids by librarians. There are many interesting websites here. HORSES and HORSEMANSHIP are two of the more than 600 subjects. Visit <www. kidsclick.org>. Is your classroom beginning to look like the Rocking S Horse Ranch? Happy Trails to You!

ANSWERS (1. Swats flies in summer and warms him in winter—area between hind legs is only part not kept warm by hair. 2. Myra Maybelle Shirley. 3. Shot in the back. 4. 22 miles.)